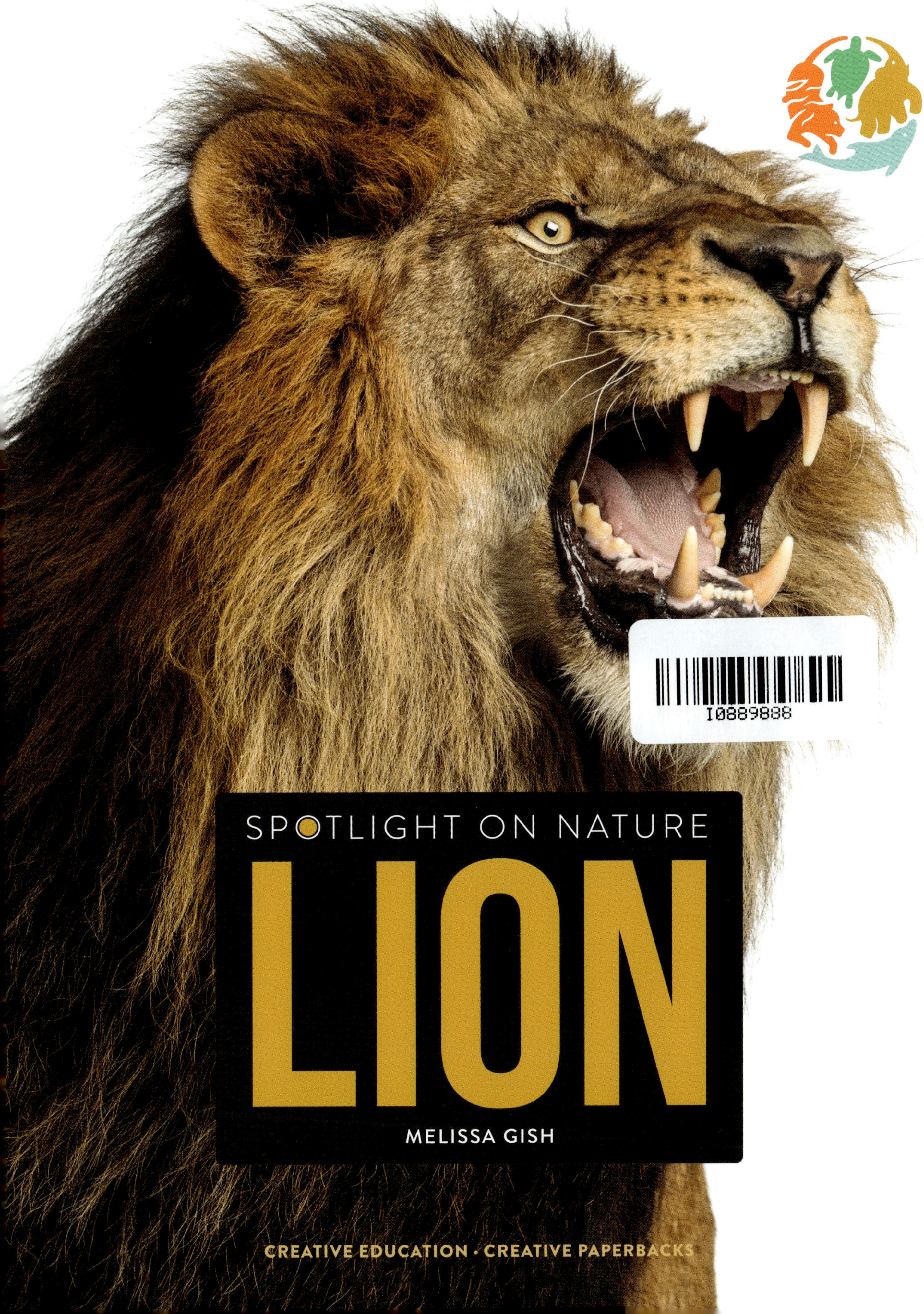

SPOTLIGHT ON NATURE

LION

MELISSA GISH

CREATIVE EDUCATION · CREATIVE PAPERBACKS

Published by Creative Education and Creative Paperbacks
P.O. Box 227, Mankato, Minnesota 56002
Creative Education and Creative Paperbacks are imprints of The Creative Company
www.thecreativecompany.us

Design by Chelsey Luther; production by Colin O'Dea
Art direction by Rita Marshall
Printed in the United States of America

Photographs by Alamy (Martin Creasser, Carole Deschuymere, Holger Ehlers, Media Drum World, Mint Images Limited, robertharding, Dave Watts), Dreamstime (Isselee), Getty Images (Brit Finucci/Moment, narasimhan/Moment, Anton Petrus/Moment), iStockphoto (AndreAnita, BreakingTheWalls, bucky_za, Eerik, GlobalP, guenterguni, KuntalSaha, RobHainer), Minden Pictures (Anup Shah/NPL), Shutterstock (Dark_Side, Edwin Godinho, Kikkia Jackson)

Library of Congress Cataloging-in-Publication Data
Names: Gish, Melissa, author.
Title: Lion / Melissa Gish.
Series: Spotlight on nature.
Includes index.
Summary: A detailed chronology of developmental milestones drives this life study of lions, including their habitats, physical features, and conservation measures taken to protect these roaring big cats.
Identifiers: ISBN 978-1-64026-340-6 (hardcover) / ISBN 978-1-62832-872-1 (pbk) / ISBN 978-1-64000-483-2 (eBook)
This title has been submitted for CIP processing under LCCN 2020902417.

First Edition HC 9 8 7 6 5 4 3 2 1
First Edition PBK 9 8 7 6 5 4 3 2 1

CONTENTS

MEET THE FAMILY
Northern Lions of Pendjari National Park 4

LIFE BEGINS 7
Featured Family
Welcome to the World 8
First Meal 10

EARLY ADVENTURES 13
Featured Family
Look Who's Lapping 14
Give It a Try 16

LIFE LESSONS 19
Featured Family
This Is How It's Done 20
Practice Makes Perfect 22

LION SPOTTING 25

Family Album Snapshots 28
Words to Know 30
Learn More 31
Index 32

MEET THE FAMILY

NORTHERN LIONS

of Pendjari National Park

Benin (*beh-NEEN*), a small West African nation, is about the size of the state of Ohio. On Benin's far northwestern edge, cheetahs, antelopes, baboons, and other animals roam the rocky cliffs, sparse forests, and grasslands of Pendjari National Park. Slicing through the park, the Pendjari River is home to hippopotamuses, crocodiles, and a variety of wading birds. This area is one of the last remaining protected habitats for elephants and lions in West Africa.

It is late November—the start of *harmattan*, the dry season named for the cool, dusty winds that blow southward from the Sahara Desert. A Northern lioness has left her family and hidden under a rocky outcropping beneath a thicket of flowering kwandari. For three and a half months, she has been carrying the developing offspring inside her body. Now, in this private place, the time has come for them to be born.

CLOSE-UP

Sharp tongues

A lion's tongue is covered with hundreds of backward-curving projections called papillae. These tiny, sharp spikes scrape meat from bones. They also help lions keep clean by combing out fur as the lion licks itself or its offspring.

CHAPTER ONE

LIFE BEGINS

Lions are members of the cat family. They are one of the four species of big cats that can roar. Baby lions, called cubs, cannot roar. It takes about two years for them to develop that ability. Lions were once divided into numerous subspecies. However, in 2017, genetic studies separated lions into just two subspecies: Southern lions and Northern lions. Southern lions are spread throughout southern and eastern regions of Africa. Northern lions are found in Central and West Africa as well as India. Since lions have adapted to diverse habitats, their appearance differs slightly, depending on where they live. For this reason, unofficial, descriptive names are often used to identify lions from different geographic regions.

PENDJARI NORTHERN LION MILESTONES

DAY 1

- Born
- Woolly fur with dark spots
- Weight: 3 pounds (1.4 kg)

FEATURED FAMILY

Welcome to the World

In Pendjari National Park, the pregnant lioness prepares to give birth. In the pale light of a half moon, three tiny cubs are born—a male and two females. Each one weighs about three pounds (1.4 kg). Their eyes are closed, and their ears are folded down. The mother lion licks them clean with her raspy tongue, fluffing their spotted fur. They can barely lift their heads. She uses a paw to pull them close to her belly, where their sense of smell helps them locate the milk she has produced for them.

Lions' bodies range from five to seven feet (1.5–2.1 m) long. Most male lions weigh about 400 pounds (181 kg). Where large prey is abundant, males may grow to nearly 500 pounds (227 kg). Females, called lionesses, are about two-thirds the size of males in their region. Slender, tufted lion tails are about three feet (0.9 m) long. Cubs begin to grow tail tufts between five and seven months of age. By the time males are about two years old, thick fur begins to cover their neck and shoulders. This fur is called a mane.

Lions live in family groups called prides. A pride consists of 2 to 20 females, their offspring, and a team, or coalition, of 2 to 10 males that protects the pride. Females work

CLOSE-UP

Flexing claws

Each of a lion's toes has a claw attached to a bone called a phalanx. This bone bends like a hinge to push the curved, one-and-a-half inch (3.8 cm) claw forward. A thumb-like dewclaw on each front paw holds down prey when eating.

10 DAYS

- Eyes and ears open
- Begin walking
- Weight: 6 pounds (2.7 kg)

3 WEEKS

- Vision improves
- Run and play with siblings

together to hunt and steal or scavenge food for the pride. Lions are carnivores, which means they eat meat. Their prey varies in size from lizards and hares to antelopes and African buffaloes weighing more than 1,000 pounds (454 kg). Cubs get their first taste of meat around three months of age. Adult lions need an average of 11 to 18 pounds (5–8.2 kg) of meat per day to survive. Males eat first, followed by females. After the hunters have eaten, cubs and old lions are allowed to eat the leftovers. Lions do not chew their food. They bite off chunks to swallow whole.

CLOSE-UP

Teeth

Born toothless, adult lions have 30 teeth. The front teeth, called incisors, grip and tear meat. The four canines can be up to four inches (10.2 cm) long. The side teeth, called carnassials, cut through meat like scissors.

FEATURED FAMILY

First Meal

In Pendjari, the lioness kept her cubs safely hidden away for eight weeks. Now about three months old, they are full-fledged pride members. The lionesses worked together in the night to bring down a young, 10-foot-tall (3 m) giraffe. With such a large kill, everyone can share in the feast without taking turns. The cubs push closer. The male, slightly bigger than his sisters, shoves them aside. He puts his new teeth to use, biting into the giraffe's warm flesh—his first taste of meat.

Adult lions need 11 to 18 POUNDS (5-8.2 KG) of meat per day to survive.

3 MONTHS

- Begin eating solid food
- Still drinking milk
- Height: 10 inches (25.4 cm) at shoulder
- Weight: 22 pounds (10 kg)

CLOSE-UP

Vision

Lions' eyes have a reflective layer of tissue called the tapetum lucidum. This tissue collects and concentrates light, giving the big cats good night vision. In low light, lions can see six times better than humans.

CHAPTER TWO

EARLY ADVENTURES

Lions can reproduce when they are about three years old. Females in a pride are usually related and may give birth at about the same time. Lionesses can have one to four cubs in a litter. Mothers will sometimes feed milk to each other's cubs, but their own offspring take priority. Some lionesses babysit the pride's cubs while the others hunt. Male lions do not help raise their young, but they do protect cubs from predators such as hyenas and jackals. When lion cubs are about three months old, they begin learning skills for adulthood. They creep slowly through the grass with their bellies close to the ground, stalking each other. They leap over rocks, chase birds, pounce on insects, and play with adults' tails.

6 MONTHS

- Spots on back fade
- Tail tassels begin to appear
- Fully weaned

1 YEAR

- Male's mane starts growing in
- Pink noses darken slightly
- Height: 28 inches (71.1 cm) at shoulder
- Weight: 155 pounds (70.3 kg)

CLOSE-UP

Speed

While chasing prey, lions can sprint up to 50 miles (80.5 km) per hour for about 200 yards (183 m). Running at full speed, a lion can generate enough energy to leap 36 feet (11 m) forward.

FEATURED FAMILY

Look Who's Lapping

Overnight, a pack of spotted hyenas invaded the Pendjari pride and snatched one of the cubs. As the sun rises, the lioness, still furious with her loss, roars angrily. She keeps her two remaining cubs close. The pride hears a herd of elephants ambling toward the river nearby. Wishing to drink before the elephants arrive, the lions trot to the riverbank. Now about seven months old, the cubs have recently been **weaned**. The parched youngsters hurry to the water's edge, hunch down, and lap up the refreshing liquid. Then their two-year-old cousin arrives. Growling in protest, they have no choice but to give way to the subadult, who is three times bigger.

LIONESSES can have ONE TO FOUR CUBS in a litter.

2 YEARS

- Subadults
- Narrow, light-colored mane visible on male
- Join hunting party

FEATURED FAMILY

Give It a Try

The Pendjari lioness has severely wounded a rock hyrax and carried it back to the pride. It weighs about 10 pounds (4.5 kg)—the perfect size for the yearling cubs to practice their hunting skills. The creature limps through the grass as the cubs encircle it, their bellies pressed to the ground. The male cub swipes at the hyrax, and it turns to bite him. The female cub leaps forward, pinning her prey to the ground.

Lions are territorial. They live in an established area and defend it from intruders. Because water attracts all sorts of animals, the best territories are close to rivers and lakes. Male lions roar to let others know that a territory is occupied. If a coalition believes it outnumbers or can overpower rivals, the group may invade a territory and try to take over. Sometimes females fight back alongside males to resist a change in leadership. The invaders will kill all the cubs in a pride in order to start their own families. Rather than allow their young to be killed, groups of females may flee a territory with their cubs until the young are safely grown.

CLOSE-UP

Ambush predators

Lions use a variety of hunting strategies. One method involves encircling prey. Some lions attack, driving the animal toward other lions that crouch unseen. These lions then leap on the prey from their hiding places.

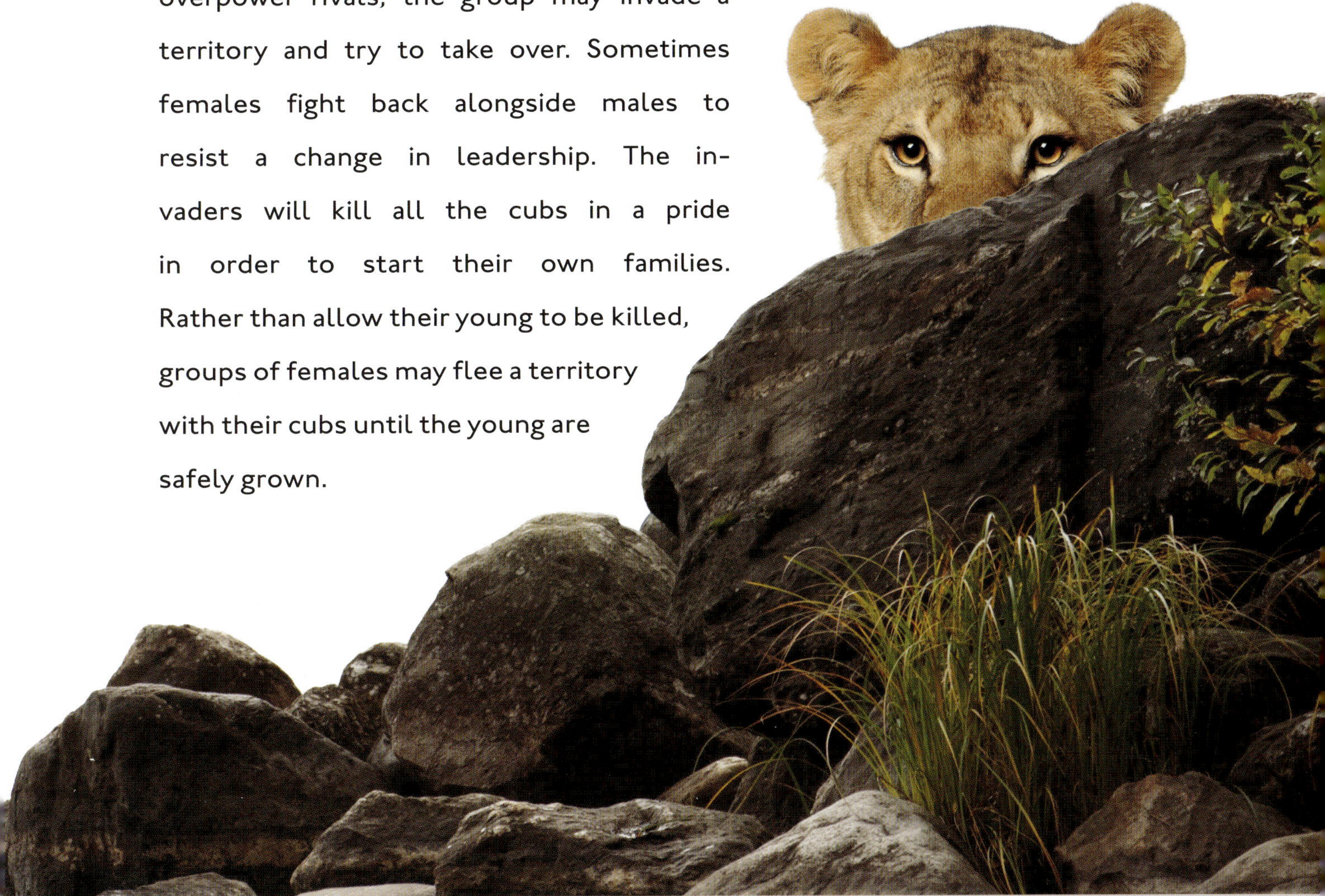

3 YEARS

- Fully mature, spots mostly gone
- Male leaves pride with half-brothers
- Height: 4 feet (1.2 m) at shoulder
- Weight: 395 pounds (179 kg)

Mane effect

Male lions usually sport a mane of fur around the neck. Manes darken and thicken with age. In the hottest habitats, male lions are maneless. In Botswana, some female lions have manes.

CHAPTER THREE

LIFE LESSONS

Lions are most active at night. They have good night vision, but they do not see any better than most of their prey. Lions approach prey with stealth, but if the wind carries the predators' scent to the prey, the hunt will be unsuccessful. About half of all attacks fail. Lions typically prefer hoofed animals, such as a wildebeest or zebra. To bring down large prey, lions attack from the side. They leap onto the animal's back and bite its neck. The goal is to sever the spine so that the prey drops to the ground. To capture smaller prey, such as an impala or duiker, a lion uses its powerful paw to smack the animal's rear end or back legs. This knocks the prey off balance. The lion then bites the throat or the snout to suffocate the animal.

4 YEARS

- Coalition establishes pride
- Spotted, dark pink nose
- Female gives birth for the first time

6 YEARS

- Male fathers cubs for the first time
- Enters strongest period of life
- Weight: 420 pounds (191 kg)

Lions must be aware of their position when hunting to avoid being stabbed by sharp horns or kicked by powerful hooves. Despite the risk of injury, lions may also attack porcupines and crocodiles. One kick from a giraffe can kill a lion, so only young giraffes are hunted. Hippos are vicious. Only when a baby hippo becomes separated from its herd will it be targeted. The first steps in learning how to become part of the pride's hunting team are playing and watching. Some youngsters hang back from hunts, waiting with the pride's male coalition for the females to deliver food. Others

CLOSE-UP

Territory

A pride's territory may be as large as 100 square miles (259 sq km). Lions travel up to 12 miles (19.3 km) per night while hunting. They stay close to water sources, since they can go only four days without water.

FEATURED FAMILY

This Is How It's Done

The Pendjari lions are now two years old. The male is larger than his sister, and a mane has started to grow around his neck. He has wandered away from the pride, following the scent of a warthog. He spots the young warthog. Catching the lion's scent, the warthog makes a dash for its underground burrow. The lion dives forward and begins digging. His sibling, attracted by the commotion, joins him in pawing dirt away from the burrow opening. The young lions won't easily give up this potential meal.

(7) **YEARS**

- Mane continues to thicken and darken
- Patchy pink-black nose

(8) **YEARS**

- Male battles with rivals
- Long, dark mane covers ears, chest, cheeks, and shoulders

FEATURED FAMILY

Practice Makes Perfect

After three years in Pendjari, the young lions have become skilled hunters and valuable members of the pride. The female will soon be ready to take on the role of motherhood, and the male will be forced out of the pride. In the cool evening, he and two other young males—his half-brothers—follow the Pendjari River southward. There, the newly formed coalition will seek out its own territory. The young lions are strong and fearless. Together, they will be able to overpower an aging male and take control of his pride.

CLOSE-UP

Scent marking

Like all cats, lions have interdigital scent glands between their toes. These produce a smell that is unique to each cat. Lions use this scent and urine to mark the boundaries of their territory.

follow along but remain hidden to watch the action.

During the first year or two of life, lionesses may give cubs small or injured prey for hunting practice. By the age of two, cubs become subadults and join the hunting party. Hunting is a vital ability for females, but young males also need to hone their skills. Males are pushed out of their original pride between ages two and three and may not establish their own prides right away. They must feed themselves while roaming in search of females to form a pride.

9 YEARS

- Enters old age
- Begins to lose weight
- Dull fur, scars, tattered ears
- Mostly black nose

12-15 YEARS

- End of life

CHAPTER FOUR

LION SPOTTING

In the wild, lions have short, difficult lives. Cubs are constantly threatened by predators such as hyenas, leopards, and male lions. Only about one in five cubs survives to see its second birthday. Male lions are usually strong enough to lead a pride only from age four to eight. After that, battles to defend the pride become too much for a lion. He weakens and succumbs to injuries or illness, or rivals kill him. Most male lions do not live more than 12 years in the wild. Females typically live a few years longer, although they may be killed while defending their cubs or hunting.

Lions everywhere are in trouble because of people. More than 80 percent of lions' native habitat has been taken over by humans, forcing more contact with people. Lions that wander outside the borders of game reserves and national parks in search of food are often killed to protect livestock. Desperately hungry lions may even attack people. Although lions kill dozens of people each year, people kill many more lions.

Since the mid-20th century, numerous protected areas have been established in Africa and Asia. But poaching, or illegal killing, of lions persists. Gir National Park and Wildlife Sanctuary, in the Indian state of Gujarat, is home to about 500 lions—the only lions in Asia. In Africa, lions are regularly poisoned or shot for their teeth, claws, and bones. Some "hunting guides" illegally lure lions outside the safety of reserve boundaries, where the lions can be killed by **trophy** hunters.

The threat to lions has reached a crisis level. Populations in some African countries have declined by nearly 50 percent in recent decades. In 2018, the government of Benin, the National Geographic Society, and several other conservation groups pledged $23.5 million to restore and protect the wilderness of Pendjari National Park. Much of the money will be used to increase law enforcement to fight the poaching of lions, elephants, and other wildlife. Similar action is being taken in other nations, including Senegal, where the Wildlife Conservation Network and the Leonardo DiCaprio Foundation fund lion conservation in Niokolo-Koba National Park. Fewer than 50 lions are believed to remain in the park, but researchers are hopeful that the population will grow with increased ranger presence. Only through education and anti-poaching efforts can people save Earth's dwindling lion populations.

FAMILY ALBUM

SNAPSHOTS

Barbary lions of North Africa were the largest lions, commonly weighing nearly 600 pounds (272 kg). These lions were hunted to **extinction** by the 1940s.

The **Northern lions** at the Rabat Zoo in Morocco are descendants of Barbary lions kept by the Moroccan royal family through the late 19th century.

The last remaining **West African lions** exist in Niokolo-Koba National Park in Senegal, which covers an area slightly larger than Puerto Rico.

The **Katanga lion**, also called Southwest African lion, is found in Angola, Botswana, Namibia, Zaire, Zambia, and Zimbabwe. Its mane is lighter than those of other lions.

Masai lions of Kenya, Ethiopia, Mozambique, and Tanzania have tufts of fur on their knee joints, and their manes appear to be combed back.

The **Transvaal lions** of South Africa's Kruger National Park and Swaziland's Hlane Royal National Park have darker manes than most other lions.

Fewer than 700 **Ethiopian lions** are believed to live in Ethiopia and Sudan, where human settlements are taking over protected wildlife areas.

Northeast Congo lions in Uganda's Queen Elizabeth National Park are among the few unique prides observed to climb and rest in trees.

Unlike other lions, **Asiatic lions** of India are divided into all-male and all-female prides. They come together only to mate.

The **Kalahari lion** is slender and lightweight, having adapted to its Kalahari Desert habitat, where temperatures can soar to 104 °F (40 °C) in the shade.

The focus of a *National Geographic* feature, the **Serengeti lion** known as C-Boy lived 14 years—the longest of any known wild male lion.

Despite being legally protected, **Somali lions** in Kenya's Arawale National Reserve are threatened because of neighboring Somalia's civil unrest and widespread poaching.

Through a breeding program begun in 2019, the Tehran Zoo hopes to reintroduce lions to the wild in Iran, where they are known as **Persian lions**.

WORDS to Know

adapted changed to improve the chance of survival in an environment

extinction the state of having died off completely

genetic of or relating to genes, the basis of physical traits inherited from parents

glands organs in an animal's body that produce chemical substances

scavenge to search for unfinished food

species a group of living beings with shared characteristics and the ability to reproduce with one another

trophy an object that is a symbol of victory or success

weaned accustomed to food other than milk

LEARN MORE

Books

Bishop, Nic. *Big Cats*. New York: Scholastic, 2019.

Roome, Hugh. *Lions: Kings of the Grasslands*. New York: Children's Press, 2019.

Simon, Seymour. *Big Cats*. Rev. ed. New York: Harper, 2017.

Websites

"African Lion." National Geographic. https://www.nationalgeographic.com/animals/mammals/a/african-lion/.

"Lion." San Diego Zoo Animals & Plants. https://animals.sandiegozoo.org/animals/lion.

"Lion." Smithsonian's National Zoo & Conservation Biology Institute. https://nationalzoo.si.edu/animals/lion.

Documentaries

Dauphin, Jean-Marc. *Growing Up in the Savannah*. Ampersand, 2015.

Rilk, Thomas. *Lionsrock: Return of the King*. ORF-Enterprise, 2012.

Steenkamp, Will, and Lianne Steenkamp. *Vanishing Kings – Lions of the Namib*. Into Nature Productions, 2015.

Note: Every effort has been made to ensure that any websites listed above were active at the time of publication. However, because of the nature of the Internet, it is impossible to guarantee that these sites will remain active indefinitely or that their contents will not be altered.

Visit

AFRICAN LION SAFARI

This drive-through park is home to more than 1,000 exotic animals.

1386 Cooper Road
Cambridge, ON N1R 5S2
Canada

THE WILD ANIMAL SANCTUARY

This sanctuary provides a 789-acre (319 ha) refuge for more than 500 lions, tigers, and other predators.

2999 County Road 53
Keenesburg, CO 80643

OUT OF AFRICA WILDLIFE PARK

Visitors can watch lions and other large carnivores eat during scheduled feeding events.

3505 W State Route 260
Camp Verde, AZ 86322

WILDLIFE SAFARI

Drive through this 600-acre (243 ha) park filled with free-roaming animals.

1790 Safari Road
Winston, OR 97496

INDEX

Africa 4, 7, 18, 26, 28, 29
birthing 4, 8, 13
conservation measures 4, 8, 10, 14, 16, 20, 22, 25, 26, 28, 29
ears 8
eyes 8, 12, 19
food 6, 8, 9, 10, 13, 14, 16, 17, 19, 20, 23, 25
fur 6, 8, 9, 18, 20, 28
India 7, 26, 29
life spans 25, 29
mating 29
movement 13, 14, 16, 17, 19, 20
offspring 4, 6, 7, 8, 9, 10, 13, 14, 16, 17, 20, 22, 23, 25
paws 8, 9, 19, 23
populations 26, 28, 29
prides 9, 10, 13, 14, 16, 17, 20, 22, 23, 25, 29
tails 9, 13
teeth 10, 26
territories 17, 20, 22, 23
threats 13, 14, 17, 20, 25, 26, 28, 29
vocalizations 7, 14, 17